Brown Bunny's Bird and Flower Book

by Barbara Mancine

illustrated by Amie Mancine

Archway Publishing books may be ordered through booksellers or by contacting:

Archway Publishing
1663 Liberty Drive
Bloomington, IN 47403
www.archwaypublishing.com
1 (888) 242-5904

ISBN: 978-1-4808-5878-7 (sc)
ISBN: 978-1-4808-5877-0 (hc)
ISBN: 978-1-4808-5879-4 (e)

Library of Congress Control Number: 2018902905

Print information available on the last page.

Archway Publishing rev. date: 3/2/2018

A little brown bunny sat in the green grass in front of a garden.

A robin hopped along the grass, looking for worms. He stopped and asked, "What are you doing, little brown bunny?"

"I am eating this delicious green grass and looking at the orange lilies," answered the bunny.

A cardinal looked down from the branches of a pine tree and asked, "What are you doing, little brown bunny?"

"I am eating this delicious green grass and looking at the pink impatiens," answered the bunny.

A goldfinch flew by, looking for seeds. He stopped and asked, "What are you doing, little brown bunny?"

"I am eating this delicious green grass and looking at the purple petunias," answered the bunny.

A nearby woodpecker, searching
for bugs, looked down and
asked, "What are you doing,
little brown bunny?"

"I am eating this delicious green grass and looking at the yellow marigolds," answered the bunny.

A chickadee, singing his
sweet birdsong, stopped and
asked, "What are you doing,
little brown bunny?"

"I am eating this delicious green grass and looking at the white daisies," answered the bunny.

"Caw, caw," said a crow from
the topmost branch of a nearby
tree. "What are you doing, little
brown bunny?"

"I am eating this delicious green grass and looking at the red roses," answered the bunny.

A hummingbird, flying from flower to flower, stopped and asked, "What are you doing, little brown bunny?"

"I am eating this delicious green grass and looking at the blue bachelor's buttons," answered the bunny.

The little brown bunny looked up at the clear blue sky and said, "I thank you, God, for the birds, the flowers, and my animal friends."

About the Author

Barbara Mancine is a retired elementary school teacher. She lives in Stow, Ohio, where she enjoys spending time with her seven grandchildren.

Amie Mancine teaches life sciences at high school and college levels at Archbishop Hoban High School in Akron, Ohio. She lives in North Canton with her husband, two sons, daughter, and pets.

CPSIA information can be obtained
at www.ICGtesting.com
Printed in the USA
LVHW070455231118
598005LV00016B/140/P

9 781480 858770